DISNEY·PIXAR

MONSTERS, INC.

EMPLOYEE HANDBOOK

"We Scare Because We Care!"

TOP SECRET

BY LISA PAPADEMETRIOU

DESIGNED BY DISNEY'S GLOBAL DESIGN GROUP

Random House 🏠 New York

For Catherine, Nancy, Vickie,
and all the other cast members
who make work a scream!

"A History of Monsters, Inc." artwork by Bud Luckey at Pixar Animation Studios.

Copyright © 2001 by Disney Enterprises, Inc./Pixar Animation Studios. All rights reserved under International and Pan-American Copyright Conventions. Published in the United States by Random House, Inc., New York, and simultaneously in Canada by Random House of Canada Limited, Toronto, in conjunction with Disney Enterprises, Inc. RANDOM HOUSE and colophon are registered trademarks of Random House, Inc. Library of Congress Control Number: 2001090223 ISBN: 0-7364-1236-0

Printed in the United States of America
October 2001
10 9 8 7 6 5 4 3 2 1

www.randomhouse.com/kids/disney

MONSTERS, INC.

CONTENTS

324 Scare Road
Monstropolis 40470
1-800-SCARE-ME

MONSTERS, INC.

WELCOME!

So you made it past the first interview, the one where we threw out all the monsters who definitely couldn't cut it at Monsters, Inc. Now all you need to do is pick out just which job you want to apply for in our organization. This handbook will help you figure out where in Monsters, Inc., you will be happiest—and where we will be happiest having you work.

Monsters, Inc., is the best-known and most respected scream collection and refinery corporation in Monstropolis. At Monsters, Inc., we carefully match every child with his or her ideal monster to produce a superior scream, which is then refined into clean, dependable energy.

At Monsters, Inc., you'll enjoy a fun, friendly atmosphere full of monsters who put the "care" in "scare." When you come to work for us, you can be certain that you're working with the most talented monsters in the business.

We power your car, we warm your home, and we light your city. Monsters, Inc., works for you . . . now it's time for you to work for us! Take the following test to see which job is right for you. Then fill out the job application. We look forward to hearing from you!

Yours truly,

Stanley Bilge
Monster Resources Department

MONSTERS, INC.

Scream-O-Meter

3 0 8 0 0 5 1

FOR THE MONSTERS, INC., EMPLOYEE

SO IT'S ALWAYS BEEN YOUR DREAM TO WORK AT MONSTERS, INC., BUT YOU AREN'T SURE EXACTLY WHERE YOU'LL FIT IN? TAKE THIS TEST AND FIND OUT.

1. YOU'RE ON THE SCARE FLOOR AT MONSTERS, INC., AND YOU NOTICE THAT A DOOR HAS BEEN LEFT OPEN. YOU WOULD MOST LIKELY:

- ⊙ a. Go tell your boss.
- ○ b. Slam the door shut and call the CDA.
- ○ c. Walk through the door to see if there's a child around to scare.
- ○ d. Close the door and search the entire building to see if a child has escaped.

2. YOU NOTICE THAT A MONSTER HAS JUST COME OUT OF A SCARE DOOR WITH A CHILD'S SOCK ON HIS BACK. YOU WOULD MOST LIKELY:

- ○ a. Scream for the CDA.
- ○ b. Grab a notebook and write down the date and time.
- ◉ c. Let the CDA take care of it while you scare another child.
- ○ d. Grab a pair of tongs and tackle the monster to get the sock off his back.

3. YOU NOTICE THAT ANOTHER MONSTER HAS BROUGHT FOOD ONTO THE SCARE FLOOR. YOU WOULD MOST LIKELY:

- Ⓜ a. Go over and quietly remind the monster that food is not allowed on the Scare Floor.
- ◯ b. Report the monster to his boss immediately.
- ◯ c. Keep scaring kids and collecting screams.
- ◯ d. Yell "FOOD ON THE SCARE FLOOR!" and tackle the monster to the ground.

4. ON YOUR DAYS OFF, YOU WOULD MOST LIKELY:

- ◯ a. Go to the movies.
- Ⓜ b. Go to the office to work—there are papers to be filed!
- ◯ c. Read *Innovations in Scaring*.
- ◯ d. Go shopping for tongs.

8

5. WHICH OF THE MOVIES LISTED BELOW WOULD YOU MOST LIKE TO SEE?

○ a. *A Far, Far Galaxy: Part 19*

○ b. *Filing Cabinets Are Your Friends*

○ c. *The Greatest Scarer on Earth*

⊘ d. *The Thing That Escaped Through the Closet Door*

6. YOUR FRIENDS WOULD MOST LIKELY DESCRIBE YOU AS:

- a. Fun.
- ○ b. A neat freak.
- ○ c. Scary.
- ○ d. Bossy.

HOW TO SCORE

Mostly a's:

You know how to follow rules but you don't need to be in the spotlight. You're lighthearted and fun. You'd be terrific as a Monsters, Inc., Scare Assistant or Receptionist, or at any job where it's important to keep those around you relaxed and happy.

Mostly b's:

You're more concerned with rules than you are with people. Provided you aren't mean, too, you would make excellent management material.

Mostly c's:

You don't think about anything other than scaring kids— and we need as many Scarers as we can get. If you're interested in a monstrously fun career, sign up as a Scarer today.

Mostly d's:

You're aggressive and bossy and like a challenge. You would make an excellent CDA agent.

MONSTERS, INC.

Employment Questionnaire

NAME: _Lu kinke_

DATE OF BIRTH: _AD 19_

YOU HAVE:
(check all that apply)

- ⊘ **Large fangs**
- ○ **Ferocious teeth**
- ⊘ **A horrifying hairstyle**
- ○ **Crablike pincers**
- ⊘ **Sharp claws**
- ○ **Spiky horns**
- ⊘ **Frightening breath**
- ⊘ **Red eyes that glow in the dark**
- ○ **Other scary features** (list here):

_____

_____

_____

_____

_____

IN YOUR SPARE TIME, YOU ENJOY:
(check all that apply)

- ○ Hiking/backpacking
- ○ Fishing
- ○ Knitting
- ⊘ Cooking
- ○ Burping
- ⊘ Playing games
- ○ Spending time with family
- ○ Scaring children
- ○ Scaring your friends
- ○ Scaring yourself

EDUCATION:

Check all of the following levels of education you have completed:

- ⊘ **Monster elementary**
- ○ **Monster middle school**
- ○ **Monster high**
- ○ **Monster U/basic scare degree**
- ○ **Monster U/Master's in Scaryocity**
- ○ **Monster U/Doctorate in Monstrosity**

ACADEMIC HONORS:

(check all that apply)

- ⊘ **Member, Phi Screama Scara**
- ○ **Member, Horror Honor Society**
- ○ **Recipient, Monster U Scream Scholarship**
- ○ **Recipient, Floyd Waternoose Memorial Fear Fellowship**

WORK EXPERIENCE:

Check any of the following areas in which you have had work experience:

_____

- ○ **Opening doors**
- ○ **Closing doors**
- ○ **Walking through doors**
- ⊘ **Sneaking through doors**
- ⊘ **Jumping over toys**
- ○ **Collecting things in cans**
- ○ **Screaming**
- ⊘ **Growling**
- ⊘ **Drooling**
- ⊘ **Gnashing your teeth**
- ○ **Other experience** (list here):

_____

_____

_____

_____

_____

_____

_____

_____

IN THE SPACE BELOW, PLEASE DESCRIBE THE MONSTER WHO HAS HAD THE GREATEST INFLUENCE ON YOUR LIFE AND EXPLAIN WHY:

Mergatiho

Great scarer

WHAT MAKES *YOU* SCARY?

All the stuff on
page 12

MONSTERS, INC.

A Memo from Waternoose

**PRESIDENT, CEO, AND SCARE GENIUS
OF MONSTERS, INC.**

MONSTERS, INC.

ROAR!

If you jumped, you aren't a monster, you're a human, and you shouldn't be reading this manual. If you laughed, then you don't take scaring seriously enough, and you shouldn't be reading this manual. If you roared back at the page . . . well, you have problems, and we don't want you in our company. But if you thought, "Yes— roar! Roar, indeed!" then Monsters, Inc., is the company for you.

We at Monsters, Inc., scare because we care. Our techniques have been perfected over the centuries. We discovered that:

- The mere hint of glowing eyes and a sharp claw reaching out from under a bed is usually enough to fill a scream canister more than halfway.

- Houses with night-lights are no-nos. Although children certainly panic at the sight of a fully lighted monster, it is usually better in the long run to let their imaginations make you seem even more horrifying than you already are.

- Dogs can make a monster look stupid. There's nothing less scary than a poor, innocent monster getting bitten on the ankle by a terrier—or worse, slobbered on by a golden retriever! Plus, dogs make noise and wake humans up.

- A messy room is a dangerous room. A monster who has a squeaky toy stuck to his foot is not scary to a child. But that same monster is very scary to his coworkers and to the Child Detection Agency, which would call a Cod 917—Toy Attachment—and shave and decontaminate that monster.

In conclusion, being a Monsters, Inc., Scarer is more than just a job. It's a way of life. It's risky, demanding work, but the rewards are tremendous. If you've got the right stuff, we want you.

Monstrously yours,

Henry J. Waternoose

Henry J. Waternoose

18

DOGS CAN MAKE A MONSTER LOOK STUPID.

CODE 917— TOY STUCK TO FOOT

A MONSTER IN THE DARK IS A SCARY MONSTER.

WATCH YOUR STEP!

FEAR IS 90% MENTAL.

ROARING SHOULD BE YOUR THING.

SCARING IS A WAY OF LIFE.

MONSTERS, INC., WANTS YOU!

MONSTERS, INC.

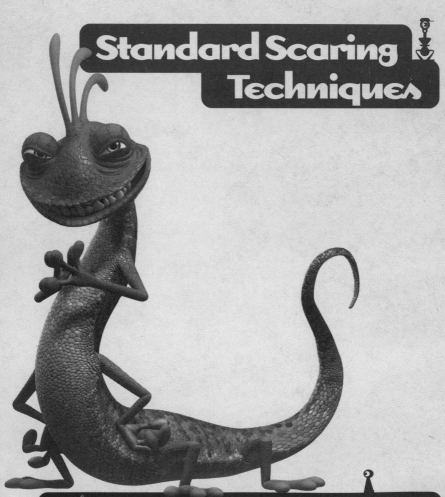

Standard Scaring Techniques

IN ORDER TO READ THIS SECTION, YOU MUST HAVE WRITTEN APPROVAL FROM MONSTERS, INC.

324 Scare Road
Monstropolis 40470
1-800-SCARE-ME

DEAR POTENTIAL SCARER,

Although we at Monsters, Inc., encourage our Scarers to develop their own personal scaring style, there are a few standard techniques that we have found very effective throughout our years in the business. Following is a list of those top techniques. Read and study this guide, and please practice these moves at home before you attend Scarer training. Remember, practice makes perfect.

Sincerely,

Ms. Flint

Ms. Flint
Scare Training Specialist

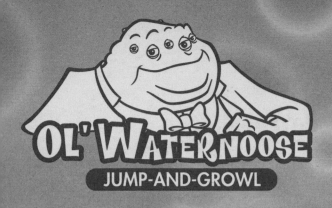

OL' WATERNOOSE
JUMP-AND-GROWL

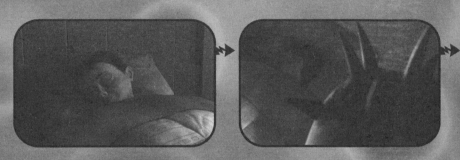

One of the oldest and most reliable scaring tactics practiced at Monsters, Inc., the Ol' Waternoose Jump-and-Growl is most effective when done quickly. Before going through the closet, grip the door handle firmly. In one quick motion, throw the door open and leap into the child's room, emitting a low growl ending with a fierce snarl.

MOST EFFECTIVE WHEN DONE QUICKLY!

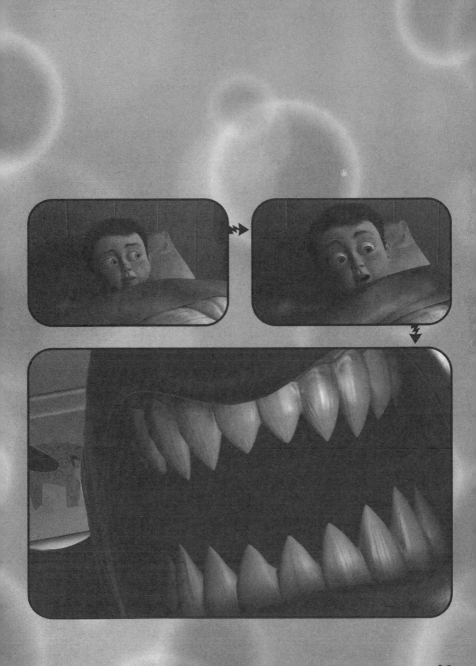

SULLIVAN
ULTRA ROAR

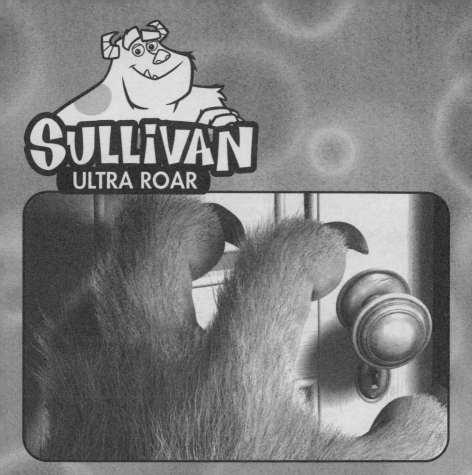

The success of this technique depends mostly on volume and timing. Wait until your child has just fallen asleep. Then open the closet door and roar as loudly as possible. Guaranteed to scare the braces off any kid.

STOP, DROP, ROLL, AND SWIPE

The Stop, Drop, Roll, and Swipe technique works best when the intended scare-ee hasn't quite fallen asleep yet. Open the closet door with a slow, creaking motion, but do not walk into the room! Instead, drop to the floor and roll under the bed. Usually, the scare-ee, suspecting that something is under his or her bed, will peer over the edge. If he doesn't, give the underside of the mattress a few gentle kicks until he leans over the bed. Then reach up quickly to expose your paw, claw, and/or tentacle.

ACTUAL CONTACT WITH ANY CHILD IS STRICTLY PROHIBITED, AS CHILDREN ARE HIGHLY TOXIC!

SPINNING VORTEX

For Scarers of smaller stature, the Spinning Vortex is the technique of choice. Spin around as quickly as possible, reaching out now and then with a claw. If the Scarer is spinning quickly enough, the intended scare-ee will not be able to tell just how small you really are.

Of course, if you are *not* spinning quickly enough, you will look ridiculous.

Boggs
QUICK REVEAL

Pioneered by Randall Boggs, this technique is most easily performed by Scarers with chameleon-like properties. However, a non-chameleon Scarer can use this technique simply by silently sneaking up behind someone and waiting for him or her to turn around. Frighteningly effective!

MONSTERS, INC.

WARNING

**The Child Detection Agency (CDA)
has issued the following warnings for all monsters:**

While a child's scream that has been refined may be powerful enough to keep the entire city of Monstropolis growling along, it is a very unstable source of energy. An unrefined scream that gets loose could result in:

- Loss of fur
- Loss of height
- Loss of car keys
- Droopy horns

- Pimples
- Good breath
- Rounded fangs

CDA Warning

In addition, be aware that there has never been a child within the city limits of Monstropolis. *It is of crucial importance that this never occur.* Contact with a child may cause any or all of the following side effects:

- Uncontrollable panic
- Fits of screaming
- Mass monsteria
- Fur loss
- Fur gain
- Melting skin
- Holes in body due to laser-beam eyes

Not only should you consider children dangerous, you should also avoid all contact with their belongings, which—since they have been exposed to the child— might contain traces of unstable scream. Following are a few common CDA terms describing situations that should be avoided:

23-19
SOCK ON THE BACK The 23 series is the common term for any article of kid clothing found on a monster. This is more than just embarrassing—it can be deadly.

917 TOY ATTACHMENT

A 900-series violation, in which a small toy gets stuck to a monster's foot, is less deadly than a 23-series violation but even more embarrassing.

57-12 MOBILE ON HEAD

Don't forget to look up. Remember that kids often have things hanging all over their rooms, and will sometimes suspend a 57-01 (kite), 57-43 (toy plane), or other object from the ceiling. A careless monster can easily walk right into one and accidentally carry it into our world.

695 ANNOYING PET

Kids often have pets, which can be just as toxic as they are—and less easily frightened. Although Monsters, Inc., tries never to send a Scarer into a house with pets, it has happened, so make sure to enter the room quickly and close the closet door immediately. Don't let these horrifying, dangerous creatures loose in our world!

3000 TOUCHED BY CHILD

The 3000 series is a class of catastrophe that even we at the CDA don't like to talk about. Therefore, we will say only this: DO NOT LET IT HAPPEN. Some children are fearless. These children must be avoided at all costs. If they touch you, there is very little we can do to help you.

If any of these situations should occur, someone on your Scare Floor should contact the CDA immediately by dialing

4357, or H-E-L-P.

One of our teams will arrive on the scene in moments to supervise any decontamination procedures that we deem necessary.

MONSTERS, INC.

A Message from George

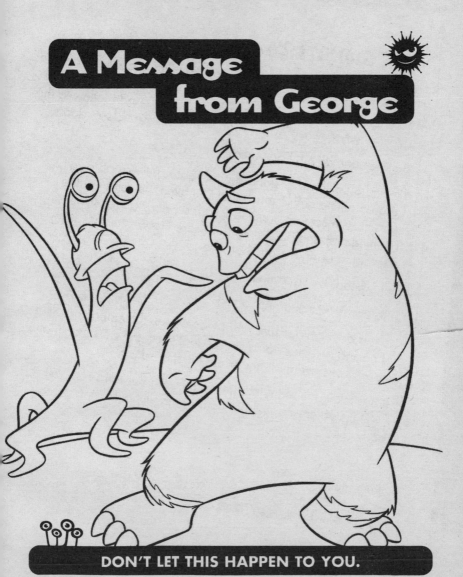

DON'T LET THIS HAPPEN TO YOU.

324 Scare Road
Monstropolis 40470
1-800-SCARE-ME

MONSTERS, INC.

ONE MONSTER'S STORY

I never thought it would happen to me. I was a dedicated Scarer. Not the best, not even close to the best. But I loved my job and tried as hard as I could to be a good Scarer. And I followed the rules. Always. I checked for night-lights. I closed closet doors.

But then one day, it happened.

I'd had a particularly good day of scaring. I was on a roll. I scared a little girl so much that she filled almost an entire canister with scream. I exited the closet door (carefully closing it behind me) and burst onto the Scare Floor, roaring for my assistant to bring me another door.

But instead, he screamed.

There was a sock on my back!

To this day, I'm not sure what was worse: the embarrassment of having my fellow Scarers see that sock, the decontamination shower, or having all my lovely fur shaved off.

It has taken me many months to recover. But I promise you this: I will never leave a child's room again without doing a complete body check.

Regretfully,

George Sanderson

George Sanderson

MONSTERS, INC.

Vacation Days and Holidays

BECAUSE EVEN THE MOST DEDICATED MONSTER
NEEDS A DAY OFF.

We at Monsters, Inc., know that sometimes monsters need vacations—perhaps a family trip to Terrorland or the Beast Coast. Our Scarers, assistants, managers, and support staff work hard and deserve some rest and relaxation. That's why we give all of our employees three weeks off every calendar year, in addition to the holidays listed below:

MONSTERS, INC.

January 12	National Horror Society Annual Picnic
February 4	Save Energy Day
February 15–17	Monster Fest
April 2	Scare Yourself Silly Day
May 23	Monster Appreciation Day
July 11	Be Anyone but Yourself Day
November 9	Monsters, Inc., Founder's Day
December 20	National Claw and Tentacle Day

All Monsters, Inc., employees are allowed unlimited sick days. More than two consecutive sick days require a doctor's note. If you are injured on the job, you will receive full pay while you recover. Simply show a doctor's note to your supervisor.

MONSTERS, INC., ALSO OFFERS FREE TREATMENT FOR THE FOLLOWING WORK-RELATED CONDITIONS:

LOSS OF ROAR:

Do you experience frequent loss of voice due to roaring and growling? Let our specialists teach you how to roar from the chest—not the throat.

CLOSET-DOOR SYNDROME:

Are your hands and elbows weak from all that closet door slamming? Our specialists will teach you the latest techniques for swinging a door shut without injuring yourself.

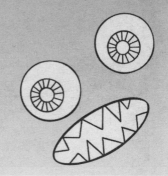

KNOTTED-FUR POX:

Is your fur all balled up from excessive tugging while scaring? Let our fur specialists show you how to condition your locks.

AND YOU CAN PURCHASE OUR PRODUCTS AT A DISCOUNT FROM THE COMPANY STORE!

MONSTERS, INC.

BECAUSE YOU ARE WHAT YOU EAT!

MONSTERS, INC.

CAFETERIA

RULES OF CONDUCT

 1. Servers will serve you. Please keep paws, claws, and/or tentacles out of the food.

 2. Do not attempt to use scaring techniques on the servers. They are not authorized to give you any more than the standard-sized portion, no matter how frightening you are.

 3. Keep it friendly. No hissing, growling, or roaring on the cafeteria line.

 4. Chameleon monsters: do not attempt to disappear before you pay for your food. If we see a tray walk out of the cafeteria by itself, we will be suspicious.

 5. Please use the knives, forks, and spoons provided. Do not place your entire face in a plate of food! This creates a mess and leads to an untidy and unprofessional appearance.

 6. Do not eat the plates and cups! We agree that they are tasty, but if we catch you eating the utensils, we will deduct the cost of the item(s) from your weekly paycheck.

Monday

Main Dish: **GRILLED SNAKE STICKS**
Side Order: **GREASY GRIMY GOPHER GUTS**
Bug Juice of the Day: **ARTIFICIALLY FLAVORED BEETLE**

Tuesday

Main Dish: **DRAGON CASSEROLE**
Side Order: **GLAZED HAIRBALLS**
Soup of the Day: **CREAM OF AARDVARK**

Wednesday

Main Dish: **FLAME-BROILED ROADKILL**
Side Order: **HUBCAPS AU GRATIN**
Dessert of the Day: **CHOCOLATE MOOSE**

Thursday

Main Dish: **SLOPPY JOES WITH MYSTERY MEAT**
Side Order: **GRUBS**
Juice of the Day: **SLIME JUICE**

Friday

Main Dish: **JUNGLE ROT PIZZA**
Side Order: **MOLD**
Vegetable of the Day: **BUGSLAW**

For those monsters who wish to leave the premises for lunch, we recommend the following restaurants:

For Lighter Fare:
TAKE A BITE

THIS LUNCH STAND OFFERS COMPLETELY UNCOOKED FOOD FOR THE BUSY MONSTER ON THE RUN. SPECIALTIES INCLUDE MIXED BUGS IN A SACK AND ROCKS ON A ROLL.

For Business Lunches:
Dine and Swill

A FULL-SERVICE MENU OFFERS SUCH DELICACIES AS ROASTED TADPOLES AND SHOE LEATHER IN HOT SAUCE. THE CHEF IS VERY ADAPTABLE AND WILL CREATE ALMOST ANYTHING TO IMPRESS YOUR GUEST.

For Fine Dining:
Dingoes at the Pier

A WATERFRONT RESTAURANT WITH A SPECTACULAR VIEW OF THE RIVER, THIS RESTAURANT SPECIALIZES IN ROASTED, FRIED, SAUTÉED, AND STEWED WILD GAME. FOR A RARE TREAT, TRY THE CORNED BEAST AND CABBAGE. IT CAN'T BE BEAT.

For Fish Lovers:
HARRYHAUSEN'S

THIS SUSHI PLACE IS ALL THE RAGE WITH MONSTERS IN THE KNOW. THE HOT-AND-SOUR SASHIMI AND GARLIC IS SAID TO GIVE AN EXTRA *OOMPH* TO THOSE MONSTERS LOOKING TO SPICE UP THEIR BREATH.

ATTENTION

MONSTERS, INC.

COFFEE BREAK

DO'S AND DON'T'S

- *Do* take time to chat with friends. Use breaks—not working hours—for socializing.

- *Don't* take hot coffee or snacks back to the Scare Floor. There's nothing scary about a monster with ice cream on his chin.

- For your own safety, *don't* feed the dispatcher.

- *Don't* gargle with milk or cream. It's for the coffee. Mouthwash is available at the company store.

- *Do* keep fur and/or tentacles away from the working parts of the cappuccino machine.

- *Do* take used cups and napkins to the recycling areas.

- *Do* throw away trash if you choose not to eat it.

- *Do* pick up a grasshopper-flavored donut from the cafeteria. They're great for dunking!

MONSTERS, INC.

A Word from Mike Wazowski

SCARE ASSISTANTS:
WHAT IT TAKES TO BE NUMBER TWO

Hi, I'm Mike Wazowski.

Do you like tough workouts? Do you enjoy doing push-ups until you think you're going to pass out? Does danger thrill you? Do you think going into a toxic child's natural habitat sounds fun and exciting?

Me neither.

Personally, I prefer telling people what to do.

And as a Scare Assistant, that's exactly what I get to do. Not that my job is easy. Scare Assistants have to:

—make sure the Scarers are in top form

—handle the precious scream canisters and make sure they get to the refinery

—handle some of the monster-sized egos of the Scarers

If bossing the big guys around sounds like fun to you, take the following quiz to see if you've got the right stuff to be a Scare Assistant.

YOU PREFER:

- ⊘ a. Lifting heavy weights.
- ○ b. Eating heavy foods.

YOU ARE:

- ⊘ a. Large and scary-looking.
- ○ b. Devilishly handsome and charming.

YOU DESCRIBE YOURSELF AS:

- ⊘ a. Strong and silent.
- ○ b. Witty and bossy.

WHEN FACED WITH DANGER, YOU:

- a. Tackle it head-on.
- b. Get someone larger than you to tackle it.

TO BE SUCCESSFUL, YOU MUST:

- a. Carry yourself with confidence.
- b. Carry a clipboard.

YOUR FAVORITE SAYING IS:

- a. "The only thing to fear is fear itself."
- b. "There's no 'I' in 'Scream Team.'"

YOU LIKE TO:

- a. Tango with danger.
- b. File goldenrod-colored paperwork.

WHEN WATCHING TV, YOU LIKE TO SEE:

⊘ a. Real-life monster police shows.

○ b. Situation comedies.

YOU LOOK MORE LIKE:

⊘ a. The Incredible Hulk.

○ b. The Incredible, Edible Egg.

Mostly a's:

Sorry, you don't seem to have what it takes to be a Scare Assistant. However, Monsters, Inc., might be able to find a place for you as a Scarer. It's not as glamorous as being an assistant, but it's a paycheck. You could do worse.

Mostly b's:

Congratulations! You're clearly already the envy of the neighborhood for your good looks and charm, and now it sounds like you've got the right stuff to be a Scare Assistant! You have a most rewarding (and important!) career ahead of you!

MONSTERS, INC.

Roz Speaks

PAPERWORK—DO IT RIGHT, OR DEAL WITH ME.

MONSTERS, INC.

LISTEN UP!

If you can't tell the difference between pink and goldenrod, don't come to work here. Paperwork, my friends, is what makes Monsters, Inc., tick. Let me break it down for you:

1. When paperwork isn't filed correctly, the system breaks down.

2. When I don't receive the Scare Reports, I have no way of knowing which children have been scared lately.

3. When I don't know who's been scared lately, we end up sending our Scarers to the same children over and over.

4. When this happens, the children gradually become less afraid of our Scarers, producing screams that are less and less powerful, until finally . . . no scream at all. Then we have to shred the door, and we can't get any more energy out of that child. Ever. Period.

If you're a Scare Assistant, just remember, I'm watching you. Always watching.

Always.

Roz

Roz

MONSTERS, INC.

Tips from a Top Scarer

**INTRODUCING JAMES P. SULLIVAN,
SCARER OF THE MONTH**

Sulley here.

Since I've been the Scarer of the Month thirty-six times in a row, they asked me to give you some tips on how to get through simulation tryouts. Just remember these five helpful hints when you're in the Simulator Room. I like to call them the ABCs of scaring.

Attire

Dress to impress. Henry J. Waternoose himself has been known to show up unexpectedly at Scarer Training, and his pet peeve is monsters who look sloppy. Well-groomed fur, clean claws, and slime-free tentacles are a must on all training days—and any day.

Basics

Focus on technique. Many trainees spend too much of their energy trying to be scary and forget to use proper form. The simulations are all about getting the basics right, like focusing on executing the Ol' Waternoose Jump-and-Growl perfectly and making sure you don't let the child see you until he or she is half asleep. You'll develop your own style as you go.

CDA

They're here for you. Sometimes Ms. Flint will try to trip up new recruits with fake CDA emergencies, such as a 23-19 (Sock on the Back) or a 695 (Annoying Pet). Study your CDA handbook before the simulation tryouts begin, so that you will know what to do. But remember—the CDA is here to keep us safe. Try to keep a level head and follow emergency procedure, and everything will be fine.

D

Door

If Ms. Flint has said it once, she's said it a hundred times: An open door is a dangerous door! It could let in a child, and none of us wants that to happen. Enter the room quickly and shut the door right away. Get in the habit now, and you'll be ready for the real thing on the Scare Floor.

E

Easy does it

Don't be afraid. In the past, some Scarer recruits have lost it at the sight of the very realistic child in the Simulator Room. Try to remember—it isn't real. It can't hurt you. Later, when you become an official Scarer, you will have to face real children. In real scare situations, you'll need to keep a cool head, which is all the more reason to try to get comfortable practicing with the simulated child now.

55

MONSTERS, INC.

Scarer of the Month

EACH MONTH, THE SCARER WITH THE LARGEST SCREAM-ENERGY COLLECTION BECOMES THE SCARER OF THE MONTH. THE PICTURE OF THE AWARD-WINNING MONSTER IS HUNG IN VARIOUS PLACES AROUND THE BUILDING FOR EVERYONE TO SEE. THIS IS A VERY IMPRESSIVE AWARD TO WIN. GOOD LUCK!

MONSTERS, INC.

Required Reading for New Employees

1. <u>THERE'S A CHILD ON MY BACK! AND OTHER TALES OF HORROR,</u>
   BY ANONYMOUS
2. <u>TOYS ARE NOT TO BE PLAYED WITH!</u>
   <u>AN ENCYCLOPEDIA OF HUMAN TOYS,</u>
   <u>BY THE CDA</u>
3. <u>FURRY CREATURES THAT ARE NOT MONSTERS:</u>
   <u>A SHORT DESCRIPTIVE MANUAL OF HUMAN PETS,</u>
   BY THE CDA

READ 'EM AND SHRIEK.

MONSTERS, INC.

Emergency Procedures

1. In the event of a fire, leave the building.

2. In the event of a flood, leave the building.

3. In the event of a tornado, hide under a large piece of furniture, unless you are too big to fit, in which case you should place the furniture on top of your head.

4. In the event of a power outage, if you are stuck inside a child's room, do not panic. An emergency team will rescue you.

5. In the event of contact with a human child or a human child's belongings, contact the CDA.

SAFETY FIRST . . . THROUGH FIFTH!

MONSTERS, INC.

A History of Monsters, Inc.

40,000 B.C.

Monsters frighten cavemen.

500 B.C.

Monsters harass ancient Greeks.

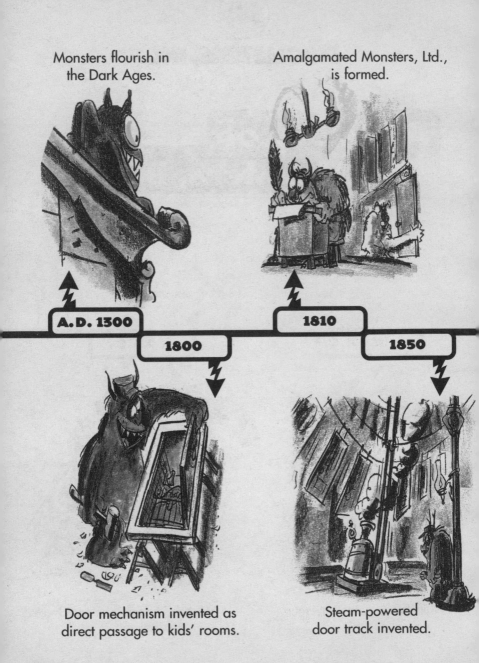

Monsters flourish in the Dark Ages.

Amalgamated Monsters, Ltd., is formed.

A.D. 1300

1800

1810

1850

Door mechanism invented as direct passage to kids' rooms.

Steam-powered door track invented.

A human named Edison invents the light bulb.

Amalgamated Monsters, Ltd., becomes Monsters, Inc.

1890

1895

1890

1900

Monsters learn how to unscrew them.

Monsters, Inc., prospers and expands facilities.

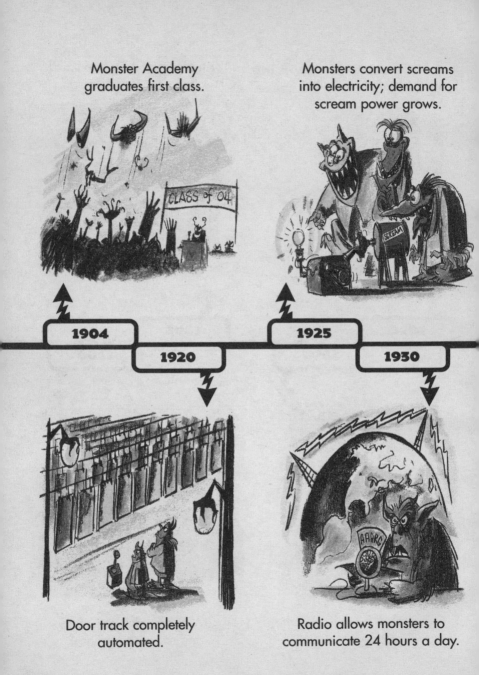

Monster Academy
graduates first class.

Monsters convert screams
into electricity; demand for
scream power grows.

1904

1920

1925

1930

Door track completely
automated.

Radio allows monsters to
communicate 24 hours a day.

Business booms and Monsters, Inc., builds new state-of-the-art facilities.

Kids focus fears on things other than monsters.

1957

1975

1970

2000

Monsters, Inc., launches own communication satellite.

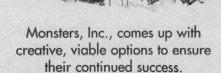

Monsters, Inc., comes up with creative, viable options to ensure their continued success.

MONSTERS, INC.

In Conclusion

We at Monsters, Inc., will continue to power Monstropolis into the next monster millennium! Being an employee of Monsters, Inc., isn't just a job, it's a time-honored tradition. Remember, at Monsters, Inc., "We Scare Because We Care!"

SEE YOU AROUND THE WATER COOLER!